PUFFIN BOOKS

INTERGALACTIC KITCHEN
GOES PREHISTORIC

The Bird family's famous space-travelling kitchen is in trouble with Mr Crabbit from the Department for the Control of Aviation Systems. He demands that the kitchen immediately takes a flight test. But on the test. But on the test a lightning strike unexpectedly sends the kitchen and its occupants back in time.

The Birds face fierce carnivorous dinosaurs, but Mr Crabbit decides he is really a caveman at heart and goes wild!

This enormously funny story, told in a highly entertaining mix of text and comic strip, is certain to win many new fans for *The Intergalactic Kitchen*.

Frank Rodgers was formerly an art teacher but is now a full-time illustrator and author. He is married with two children and lives in Glasgow.

By the same author

THE INTERGALACTIC KITCHEN
RICKY ZEDEX AND THE SPOOKS
TEACHERS ARE CREATURES

THE INTERGALACTIC KITCHEN GOES PREHISTORIC

Written and illustrated by
FRANK RODGERS

PUFFIN BOOKS

PUFFIN BOOKS

Published by the Penguin Group
Penguin Books Ltd, 27 Wrights Lane, London W8 5TZ, England
Penguin Books USA Inc., 375 Hudson Street, New York, New York 10014, USA
Penguin Books Australia Ltd, Ringwood, Victoria, Australia
Penguin Books Canada Ltd, 10 Alcorn Avenue, Toronto, Ontario, Canada M4V 3B2
Penguin Books (NZ) Ltd, 182–190 Wairau Road, Auckland 10, New Zealand

Penguin Books Ltd, Registered Offices: Harmondsworth, Middlesex, England

First published by Viking 1991
Published in Puffin Books 1993
10 9 8 7 6 5 4 3 2 1

Text and illustrations copyright © Frank Rodgers, 1991
All rights reserved

The moral right of the author has been asserted

Printed in England by Clays Ltd, St Ives plc
Filmset in Palatino

The postman was puzzled.

He had delivered all sorts of mail to Mr and Mrs Bird and family over the years, but this parcel was the oddest he had ever seen.

It was wrapped in strange, metallic paper and seemed to vibrate slightly in his hand.

Mrs Bird studied the postmark.

Mr and Mrs Krspltx were aliens whom the Birds had met when their famous intergalactic kitchen had flown into deepest space.

Attached to the parcel was a note, which said:

Dear B.B., we thought you would like this instead of a postcard. Hope you do. Please give our love to your family.
From... Mr & Mrs KRSPLTX.

B.B.'s brothers and sister, Jay, Robin and Snoo, gathered round excitedly as she opened the parcel.

As the last piece of wrapping came off, a furry shape shot out and hovered in the air in front of them. Before anyone could say anything, it spoke!

My name is GRFF. I am a robot toy module. A replica of a member of the family URSIDAE. Or, in other words...

A TEDDY! A *GREEN* TEDDY!

EXACTLY!

All the family were delighted, except Mr Bird. He didn't like robots.

THERE'LL BE TROUBLE... YOU MARK MY WORDS!

BUT DAD... GRFF IS LOVELY. HE'LL BE NO TROUBLE AT ALL!

JUST REMEMBER THAT THE KITCHEN WAS NEARLY DEMOLISHED BY A ROBOT WHEN WE WERE ALL OUT IN SPACE.

OH, ALBERT, WHAT A FUSS! I THINK YOU MUST HAVE GOT OUT OF BED ON THE WRONG SIDE THIS MORNING.

SIGH! I THINK YOU ARE RIGHT, EMILY. PERHAPS GRFF WILL MAKE ME CHANGE MY OPINION OF ROBOTS.

9

But, unfortunately, GRFF wasn't a very reliable robot. It seemed that his sensors had not appreciated the trip from his planet, because they kept going wonky. First, his direction-finder started to malfunction and the little bear careered around the kitchen out of control.

Luckily, Robin was wicket-keeper for the school cricket team and made a spectacular catch just as GRFF was about to shoot straight out of the window like a little green rocket.

Then GRFF's voice-simulator started to play tricks by leaving out the letter E.

B.B. patted the little bear on the back.

But Mrs Bird was wrong, because just then the bell rang and on the doorstep was a rather severe-looking man.

I AM CRABBIT, OF CADS, THE DEPARTMENT for the CONTROL of AVIATION SYSTEMS⊗. MAY I COME IN?

OH ... YES, PLEASE DO.

⊗DCAS, of course... but smart people like anagrams!

Mr Crabbit came in and stood stiffly to attention. He was the kind of official who enjoyed occasions like this when he could read out the rules and generally boss people about. You know the sort.

13

However, before Mr Crabbit could continue with his questionnaire, GRFF's direction-finder malfunctioned again and he shot into the air, out of control.

15

Mr and Mrs Bird hurriedly checked all the controls in the kitchen, then turned to Mr Crabbit.

"Very well," sighed Mr Crabbit, "you may begin." Mrs Bird stepped forward and pressed the ON button.

As graceful as a brick swan, the kitchen rose into the air above BONCE* (the National Bureau of Clever Experts, where Mr Bird was Janitor).

* Another "smart people" anagram!

Mr Crabbit consulted his rule-book and asked for the kitchen to perform certain manoeuvres.

FAST TURN . . .   LOOP THE LOOP . . .

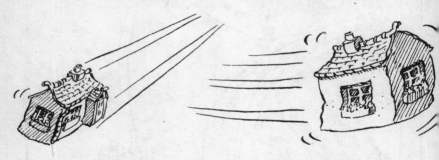

POWER DIVE . . .   EMERGENCY STOP . . .

SPIRAL . . .   and BUNNY HOP.

Mr Crabbit frowned. Everything seemed to be going too well!

Then it started to rain.

Mr Crabbit smirked as he noted down:

He shuddered as he watched the rain trickle down the windowpane.

"I hate the natural world," he said. "Give me a nice, cosy, air-conditioned office any day of the week."

Mr Crabbit made some more notes, then turned to Mr and Mrs Bird.

THE TESTS ARE ALMOST COMPLETE. SO, BEFORE I MAKE MY DECISION, HAVE YOU ANYTHING TO SAY?

Both Mr and Mrs Bird opened their mouths to reply, but before they could there was a huge clap of thunder . . .

B..B...BANG!

. . . followed by a flash of lightning . . .

CRACK!

. . . and when the family looked round they saw that Mr Crabbit had fainted.

Mr Crabbit had fainted only twice before in his life. The first time was when he accidentally took a deep breath of fresh air and the second was when his calculator broke down and he realized he would have to do some adding up on his own.

I WORKED OUT ONCE WHAT WOULD HAPPEN IF THE PROTECTIVE SCREEN WAS STRUCK BY LIGHTNING. NOW, WHAT WAS IT?

Mr Bird was about to find out, because just then . . .

The kitchen was filled with a
blinding light. Everyone shut
their eyes, then felt a slight
judder as if the kitchen were a
car that had bumped on to the
pavement.

A few seconds later everyone blinked and opened their eyes.

Slowly, Mr and Mrs Bird brought the kitchen down to the level of the tree-tops to get a better look. But as they did . . .

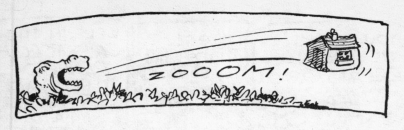

ZOOOM!

WHAT ON EARTH WAS THAT?

Jay consulted his book, *One Million Useful Facts*, and discovered something startling.

THAT WAS A *TYRANNOSAURUS REX!* A FLESH-EATING DINOSAUR THAT LIVED AROUND 100 MILLION YEARS AGO!

NOW I REMEMBER! I CALCULATED THAT IF A LIGHTNING BOLT HIT THE PROTECTIVE SHIELD THEN THE ENERGY SURGE COULD PROBABLY SEND THE KITCHEN *BACK IN TIME!*

YOU MEAN ... WE ARE IN *PREHISTORIC TIMES??*

Yes! That's what my sensors were saying!

WE'RE IN THE *CRETACEOUS PERIOD* TO BE EXACT! 135 TO 65 MILLION YEARS AGO.

AND WE COULDN'T HAVE PICKED A WORSE PERIOD! AS WELL AS TYRANNOSAURUS REX THERE ARE ALLOSAURUS, TARBOSAURUS, AND GORGOSAURUS. ALL CARNIVOROUS DINOSAURS!

I'M GOING TO GET A BAG OF BISCUITS TO FEED THE SORRUSES!

HADN'T WE BETTER LAND AND FIND OUT WHERE WE ARE?

GOOD IDEA, SNOO. LANDING POSITIONS EVERYONE!

Everyone held on to something solid as Mr Bird
gently landed the kitchen in a clearing.
Apprehensively they opened the door and stepped
out on to the Earth as it was 100 million years ago!

30

But before GRFF could impress Mr Bird with his technical expertise, his direction-finder went wrong again and he took off like a skyrocket.

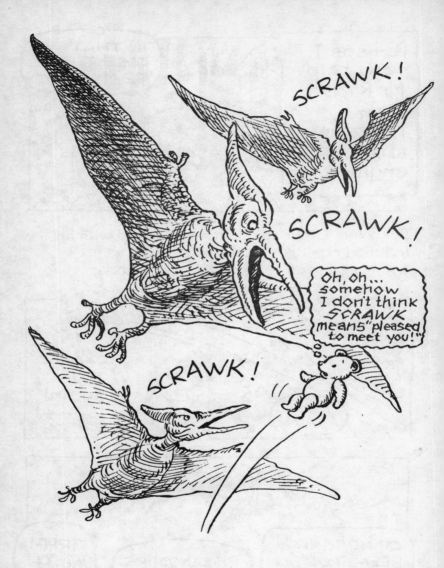

With harsh cries the huge Pteranodons beat their leathery wings and swooped towards GRFF, their sharp beaks wide open in anticipation of a new kind of lunch.

Just as they were about to snap him out of the sky, GRFF's flight path changed abruptly and he shot back down again towards the kitchen, with the bird-reptiles in hot pursuit.

Before they could turn and run for cover into the kitchen there was a blood-curdling scream behind them . . .

. . . which frightened the Pteranodons into turning tail and flying off, leaving GRFF to land safely. Then, as everyone turned towards the kitchen, they were confronted by a strange sight.

34

The trip back in time had unlocked the "wild man" that had always lurked in the back of Mr Crabbit's brain. Now it was free, and with another joyous yell (which he thought was like King Kong but was in fact more like a Country and Western singer) he rushed past the startled Birds into the jungle.

The family dashed after him . . .

. . . but lost sight of him in the dense undergrowth.

Mr and Mrs Bird called a halt and gathered everyone together.

Cautiously everyone crept inside.

It was Mr Crabbit . . . caveman!

He was getting rid of all his pent-up dislike for
his job by drawing pictures of his office colleagues
with assorted weaponry embedded in their bowler
hats.

These drawings were discovered 100 million
years later and to this day some people believe that
mankind is descended from a fierce, warlike race of
prehistoric City gents.

Mr Crabbit's answer to that was a deafening . . .

AAA-EE-AAH!!

. . . and before the startled Birds could recover, he rushed past them out of the cave.

But Mr Crabbit's high-pitched yodel had disturbed some loose rocks and down they came . . .

When the dust settled, they saw that the cave entrance was blocked by fallen rocks, jammed so tightly together that they couldn't be moved.

The Birds sat down and waited . . . and waited.
They had almost given up hope when, suddenly,
they heard a huge roar outside and GRFF shot back
through the opening.

Everyone dived for cover as outside they heard
the thunder of huge feet getting closer. Then . . .

The rocks blocking the entrance were scattered like ninepins. The angry dinosaur looked through the opening but, luckily, didn't see the Birds.

Growling in annoyance, it turned on its heel and lumbered off to bathe its sore head in the river. Cautiously, everyone came out into the open.

They were all impressed, including Mr Bird. But before he could say "Thank you", a small rock, loosened by the Triceratops's charge, fell from the mouth of the cave and bounced off GRFF's head. The little bear dropped to the ground and lay motionless.

B.B. was soundly hugged by everyone and it was decided to take GRFF back to the kitchen and try to work out a plan to rescue Mr Crabbit and get back to their own time.

As they went, the children picked up some "souvenirs".

Suddenly, they heard an ear-splitting but familiar sound above them.

As Mr Crabbit swung past, a giant head reared up from behind some trees.

Luckily for Mr C., as he swung up he hit the monster right on the nose . . .

. . . knocking its head clean off its shoulders!

The intrepid bowler-hatted Tarzan was so amazed that he let go of the rope and fell on top of the dinosaur, knocking himself out.

When the family rushed up moments later, they were confronted by an extraordinary sight.

"It must be an alien spy robot," said Snoo.

"Just think," said Jay, "robots were on the Earth before man arrived!"

Mr Bird sniffed in disdain. He didn't like the idea of robots being his ancestors. He examined the back of the robot and found a hatch.

While Mr and Mrs Bird disconnected the power pack, Snoo, Robin, Jay and B.B. made a Red Indian-style litter for Mr Crabbit.

Soon they were off again, following the trail of B.B.'s biscuits . . .

. . . which led right to the door of the kitchen. (B.B. was secretly disappointed that the dinosaurs hadn't eaten any of the biscuits and decided to try chocolate instead of plain next time.)

Once inside, the children put their "souvenirs" in a cupboard and laid Mr Crabbit beside GRFF.

Snoo was the best climber so she quickly shinned up a tall tree and scanned the skies.

Snoo went down the tree as if it were a greasy flag-pole.

Snoo, Jay and Robin dashed back to the kitchen and slammed the door behind them as the spaceship fired a laser beam.

Mrs Bird plugged in the final connection to the
power pack.

Everyone crossed their fingers as Mrs Bird
pressed the start button. Slowly the kitchen lifted off.
Then, gathering speed, it shot up into the sky . . .

. . . straight towards the spaceship!

But just as they collided, the time-boost was
activated in the kitchen.

Inside the kitchen, everyone was shaken but unhurt by the jolt and explosion of light. They rushed to the windows.

Mr Bird's relief at having given the trigger-happy robots the slip was short-lived, however, because just then Snoo saw something.

There it was, small and slightly battered. It squatted on the table, trembling slightly, like a huge, discarded toy whose batteries had almost given out.

They didn't have time to examine it because, at that moment, Mr Crabbit woke up.

Helped by Jay and Robin, he got to his feet shakily and looked out of the window.

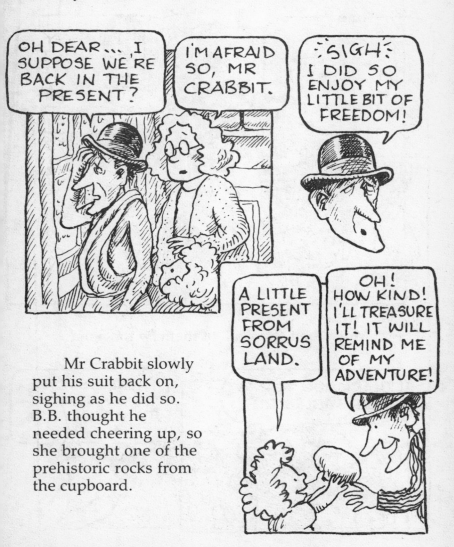

OH DEAR.... I SUPPOSE WE'RE BACK IN THE PRESENT?

I'M AFRAID SO, MR CRABBIT.

:SIGH: I DID SO ENJOY MY LITTLE BIT OF FREEDOM!

A LITTLE PRESENT FROM SORRUS LAND.

OH! HOW KIND! I'LL TREASURE IT! IT WILL REMIND ME OF MY ADVENTURE!

Mr Crabbit slowly put his suit back on, sighing as he did so. B.B. thought he needed cheering up, so she brought one of the prehistoric rocks from the cupboard.

A few moments later, the kitchen landed back at the house.

Mr Crabbit shook all of them by the hand.

THANK YOU FOR A MEMORABLE TRIP.

THERE IS ONE THING I HAVE TO DO BEFORE I GO.

He rummaged in his briefcase and brought out two large documents. He signed both and gave one to Emily and one to Albert.

He smiled wryly as he walked to the door. "Test flights just won't be the same after this," he said.

As the door closed behind Mr Crabbit, there was a strange noise from the kitchen table.

A ladder appeared and down it climbed two little robots.

The robots looked shamefaced.

They explained that they came from a far-off planet where they had been part of an experiment to travel in time. They had journeyed backwards 100 million years by mistake and then discovered that they could not return.

Mr Bird raised his eyes and shook his head.

Suddenly LRL gave a shout of recognition.

LRL pointed straight at GRFF! Both robots
jumped off the table and ran over to the lifeless bear.

FROM THE SAME PLANET?? WHAT AN *INCREDIBLE COINCIDENCE!*

To show you how rare these incredible coincidences are, here are the only other two incredible coincidences that occurred in the Universe that day.

GREETINGS FROM EARTH. MY NAME IS BERT.

SO IS MINE!

WAITER! THERE'S A *BEAVER* IN MY SOUP!

Meanwhile, LRL and HRDY were studying GRFF.

He is very quiet. What's wrong?

HE'S BROKEN. CAN YOU FIX HIM?

Of course!

HRDY ran back to the spaceship and returned
with a strange little device which he placed over
GRFF's head. A soft humming sound came from it.

Suddenly GRFF sat up.

To prove that he was
OK, GRFF flew into the
air and performed some
nifty aerobatics.

When he landed again, he recognized the two robots.

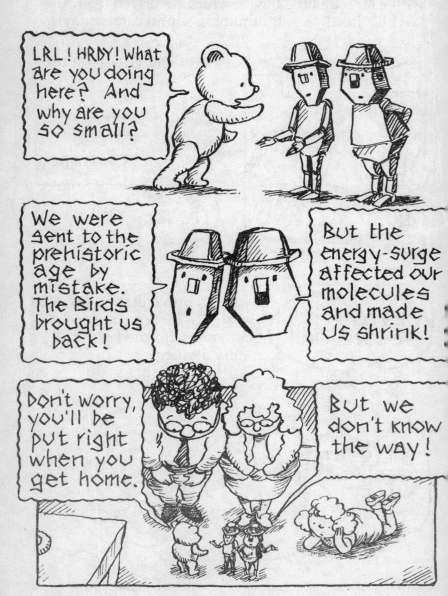

LRL! HRDY! What are you doing here? And why are you so small?

We were sent to the prehistoric age by mistake. The Birds brought us back!

But the energy-surge affected our molecules and made us shrink!

Don't worry, you'll be put right when you get home.

But we don't know the way!

GRFF, LRL and HRDY climbed aboard the spaceship.

The door closed and almost immediately the engines started. The little spaceship quivered on the table, then slowly lifted off, turned and headed for the kitchen door.

Once outside, it raced into the sky and quickly disappeared from sight.

Back inside the kitchen, B.B. sat down at the table and looked glum.

Mr Bird was secretly relieved. He was still convinced that robots meant nothing but trouble and was looking forward to a nice, quiet life now that they had gone.

Which only goes to prove that you should "never count your chickens", because just then the phone rang.

The children dashed over to the cupboard that held their "souvenirs" and discovered that their "rocks" had hatched too!

BABY DINOSAURS!!

THEY ARE PROTOCERATOPS! QUITE SMALL FOR DINOSAURS, REALLY. THEY WILL ONLY GROW TO BE SIX AND A HALF FEET LONG!

THE SAME SIZE AS A HORSE! WE COULD BUILD THEM A STABLE!

"Great idea!" replied Snoo, Robin and Jay.

Emily smiled and turned to Albert.

"I think so too," she said. "What do you think, Albert?"